The Many Adventures of Pig Batter

Goes on a Plane

The Many Adventures of Pig Batter

Goes on a Plane

Robert Czubinski

Illustrations by: Amber Czubinski

ReadersMagnet, LLC

ReadersMagnet, LLC
10620 Treena Street, Suite 230 | San Diego, California, 92131 USA
1.619.354.2643 | www.readersmagnet.com

Book design copyright © 2021 by ReadersMagnet, LLC. All rights reserved.
Cover design by Kent Gabutin
Interior design by Renalie Malinao

Hello Pig Batter what's the matter? Today is Monday it is going to be a nice day.

I am going on a plane

MONDAY
FLY OUT
TO SEE
DEVIN 2

We arrived at the airport
and felt a little funny, like I
had a circus running inside my
tummy.

TAXI

Here I sit at the airplane's gate, I am so excited I just cannot wait!

FLIGHT 129
NOW BOARDING

As I file into the large triple seven, I think of how fast it will take to see my friend Devin.

The craft is going down the runway so fast, it shakes and rubles soon were off with a blast.

Looking out the window I can see clouds like cotton, things below are so small like there is not a bottom.

The nice lady gave me a
snack of juice and nuts,
something very simple to sit in
our guts.

APPLE
JUICE

The time is coming soon I surely can feel, we bumped and swooped with a tug at the wheel.

We pulled right up to the well-lit gate, I am coming Devin it's time to celebrate.

Happy
Birthday!

The captain and flight
attendant give us a wave,
and wish us all to have a nice
day.